# The Tree That Bear Climbed

by Marianne Berkes
illustrated by Kathleen Rietz

These are the roots
that anchor the tree
that bear climbed.

This is the soil
that feeds the roots
that anchor the tree
that bear climbed.

This is the rain
that waters the soil
that feeds the roots
that anchor the tree
that bear climbed.

This is the trunk
that stands in the rain
that waters the soil
that feeds the roots
that anchor the tree
that bear climbed.

These are the branches
that stretch from the trunk
that stands in the rain
that waters the soil
that feeds the roots
that anchor the tree
that bear climbed.

These are the leaves
that grow from the branches
that stretch from the trunk
that stands in the rain
that waters the soil
that feeds the roots
that anchor the tree
that bear climbed.

This is the sun
that shines on the leaves
that grow from the branches
that stretch from the trunk
that stands in the rain
that waters the soil
that feeds the roots
that anchor the tree
that bear climbed.

These are the blossoms
that bloom in the sun
that shines on the leaves
that grow from the branches
that stretch from the trunk
that stands in the rain
that waters the soil
that feeds the roots
that anchor the tree
that bear climbed.

This is the pollen
deep in the blossoms
that bloom in the sun
that shines on the leaves
that grow from the branches
that stretch from the trunk
that stands in the rain
that waters the soil
that feeds the roots
that anchor the tree
that bear climbed.

These are the bees
that gather the pollen
deep in the blossoms
that bloom in the sun
that shines on the leaves
that grow from the branches
that stretch from the trunk
that stands in the rain
that waters the soil
that feeds the roots
that anchor the tree
that bear climbed.

This is the hive
that's home to the bees
that gather the pollen
deep in the blossoms
that bloom in the sun
that shines on the leaves
that grow from the branches
that stretch from the trunk
that stands in the rain
that waters the soil
that feeds the roots
that anchor the tree
that bear climbed.

This is the honey
made in the hive
that's home to the bees
that gather the pollen
deep in the blossoms
that bloom in the sun
that shines on the leaves
that grow from the branches
that stretch from the trunk
that stands in the rain
that waters the soil
that feeds the roots
that anchor the tree
that bear climbed.

This is the bear
who ate the honey
made in the hive
that's home to the bees
that gather the pollen
deep in the blossoms
that bloom in the sun
that shines on the leaves
that grow from the branches
that stretch from the trunk
that stands in the rain
that waters the soil
that feeds the roots
that anchor the tree
that he climbed!

The bees were not happy and neither was bear!

# For Creative Minds

## Basic Needs of Plants

**sunlight and heat (temperature and food)** — **rain (water)** — **soil (nutrients and space)** — **seed dispersal or pollination**

All living things live in habitats that meet all of their basic needs. Animals need food, water, oxygen to breathe, and a safe space for shelter and for giving birth to their young. Plants have basic needs too:

Different types of plants need different temperatures (heat) and light. Both of these needs are met by the sun. Plants that grow near the poles or at high altitudes survive cold temperatures. Plants that grow in the tropics need hot temperatures.

All plants need water. Water comes from rain or snow (precipitation). Some plants, like those found in the rainforests, need a lot of water. Other plants, like those found in the desert, do not need very much water.

Soil is made of lots of small pieces of rocks (mineral), and decayed plants and animals (organic)—nutrients for the plants. Different plants need different kinds of soil. Some plants live better in sandy soil (beaches or deserts) and other plants need thick, rich soil (forests or grasslands).

Plants also need room to grow. Roots need to spread out and leaves need to be able to reach sunlight.

Many plant seeds disperse away from parent plants so they will have their own space to grow.

# Plant Body Part Matching Activity

Match the plant body part to its description and what it does.

You usually can't see roots because they are mostly underground. Roots anchor the plant in the ground and absorb water and nutrients. The roots protect the soil from washing away (erosion). When the plants die, they decay and the pieces of the old plant are added to the soil as nutrients.

Stems are the "backbone" of the plant. They can be hard (like tree trunks) or bendable (tulips), but they are what hold up the plants. Stems move water and nutrients from the roots to the leaves.

Leaves act as "solar panels" for the plants. They turn and reach to get as much sunlight as possible. They use the sunlight, water, carbon dioxide (from the air) and the green in the leaves (chlorophyll) to make food through a process called photosynthesis. Leaves release oxygen into the air. We need this oxygen to breathe.

Flowers are not just pretty to look at—they are also the part of the plant that makes more plants. Flowers make seeds that have to be spread (dispersed) so they can grow into seedlings. The flowers attract animals to pollinate them. After the flower is pollinated, the flower grows in a fruit with seeds inside. Not all fruits are edible.

Fruits are coverings that protect the seeds.

# How Plants and Animals Interact

All plants come from seeds. Plants need animals, wind, and water to disperse seeds away from the parent plant so the seed has its own space to grow into a new plant. Fruit-eating animals leave seeds behind when they go to the bathroom. Squirrels store nuts for the winter. Some of those nuts will be forgotten and will grow into new trees. Some seeds get stuck in animal fur and are carried to another location where they can grow. Wind and water carry some seeds away from parent plants too.

Plants don't have mouths as we do, but they do need food to grow. Green plants use carbon dioxide, sunlight, and water to make sugars. These sugars are the food that help the plants grow. This process (photosynthesis) makes the oxygen that we and other animals breathe.

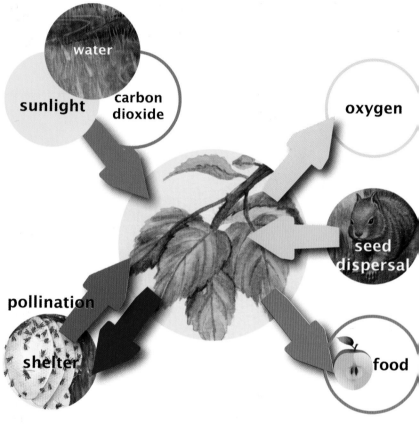

Plants use sunlight and water to make their own food through photosynthesis. They are the bottom or the beginning of the food web in any habitat. Herbivores are animals that only eat plants. Carnivores eat other animals. But carnivores still rely on plants to have fed the animals they eat, earlier in its food chain.

Many animals use plants for shelter. Birds build nests out of plant materials, often in a tree or other type of plant. Bees build their hives in plants and need the pollen from flowers to make honey.

Many plants rely on animals for pollination. Animals move pollen within a single plant as they eat or from one plant to another as they travel from plant to plant.

The flowers attract the animals with their bright colors, their scents, or both. Bees, bats, butterflies, moths, and beetles are all animals that help pollinate different plants.

Humans use plants, too! We use plants for food, houses, clothing (cotton and linen), and even medicines.

# Hands On: Plant Experiments

We eat all kinds of fruits. In fact, many of the plants we think of as vegetables are actually fruit because they are the covering for seeds. Scientifically, tomatoes, cucumbers, peppers, and squash are all fruits not vegetables. For the next week, look for the seeds in the fruits (and vegetables) you eat. Do you eat the seed(s) or do you cut the seeds out and throw them away?

Plants help keep soil in place. Take a cup of water and pour it on the ground outside in a place where there are many plants, like grass. Next, take another cup of water and pour it on the ground outside in a place where there are no plants, like in a sandbox. What happens to the ground when the water flows over it? How do you think plants help keep soil in place?

How do stems carry water? In a small cup, combine water with a little food coloring. Cut a piece of celery and place it upright in the water. How long does it take the colored water to get to the top of the celery? Cut the celery in half to see the xylem tubes that carry the water.

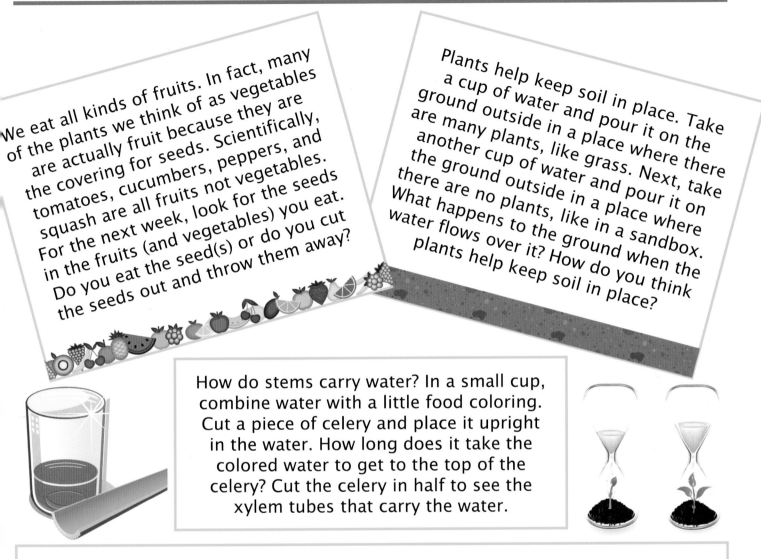

If you have potted plants in your house, you probably already know that you need to water them. After all, water is a basic need of plants (and animals). What would happen to a plant if you didn't water it? Take some seedlings (you can plant your own in paper cups or, depending on the time of year, you can buy some inexpensive seedlings already in containers) and experiment with what might happen if a plant's basic needs are not met. Some variables include:

Plant seeds in different types of soil (sand, gravel, top soil, clay, etc.).

Change the temperature (cold, cool, warm, hot).

Change the amount of and/or the length of light (bright light, low light).

Change the amount of water.

Plant seeds in different sizes of containers (space).

For Trish Purdham and June Parrilli, media specialists extraordinaire! Love, M.B.
For Leon—KR
Thanks to Lisa Davis, Associate Director of Education at the Denver Botanic Gardens, for reviewing the accuracy of the information in this book.

Berkes, Marianne Collins.
The tree that bear climbed / by Marianne Berkes ; illustrated by Kathleen Rietz.
p. cm.
Summary: Through rhyming text reminiscent of "The House that Jack Built," tells of a tree, from the roots that anchor it in the soil to the bear who climbs its trunk to snack on honey from a beehive high in its branches. Includes facts about plants.
ISBN 978-1-60718-528-4 (hardcover) -- ISBN 978-1-60718-537-6 (pbk.) -- ISBN 978-1-60718-546-8 (english ebook) -- ISBN 978-1-60718-555-0 (spanish ebook)  [1. Stories in rhyme. 2. Trees--Fiction. 3. Bears--Fiction.] I. Rietz, Kathleen, ill. II. Title.
PZ8.3.B4557Tre 2012
[E]--dc23
2012003745

Also available as eBooks featuring auto-flip, auto-read, 3D-page-curling, and selectable English and Spanish text and audio ISBN: 978-1-60718-565-9

Hardcover Spanish translation—El árbol que trepó el oso—ISBN: 978-1-60718-679-3

Interest level: 003-008; Grade level: P-3; Lexile Level: 450L

Curriculum keywords: plant adaptations and parts, basic needs, photosynthesis, plants, repeated lines, rhythm or rhyme, sun light/heat

Manufactured in China, June, 2012
This product conforms to CPSIA 2008
First Printing
Sylvan Dell Publishing
Mt. Pleasant, SC 29464